D0615100
THE
SHOW-AND-TELL
WAR

Also by Janice Lee Smith

The Monster in the Third Dresser Drawer

And Other Stories About Adam Joshua

The Kid Next Door and Other Headaches

Stories About Adam Joshua

It's Not Easy Being George

Stories About Adam Joshua (And His Dog)

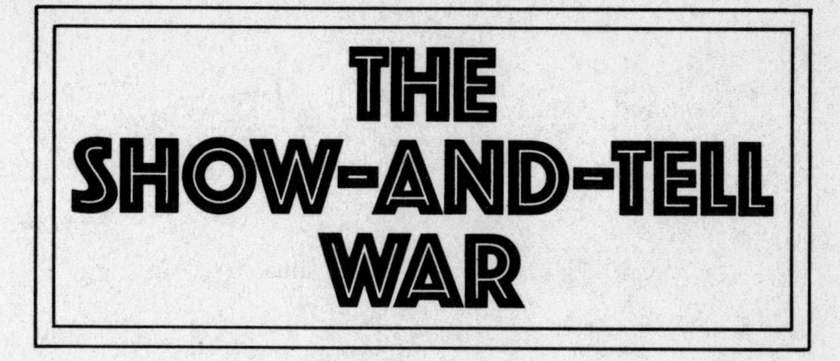

And Other Stories About Adam Joshua

by Janice Lee Smith
drawings by Dick Gackenbach

A Harper Trophy Book
Harper & Row, Publishers

The Show-and-Tell War and Other Stories About Adam Joshua

Library of Congress Cataloging-in-Publication Data
Smith, Janice Lee, 1949–
The show-and-tell war and other stories about Adam Joshua.

Summary: Five stories relate the adventures and misadventures of Adam Joshua as he contends with the first day of school, pretending to be sick, stealing a library book, making the scariest Halloween costume, and being upstaged at show-and-tell time.
[1. Humorous stories] I. Gackenbach, Dick, ill.
II. Title.
PZ7.S6499Sh 1988 [Fic] 85-45842
ISBN 0-06-025814-4
ISBN 0-06-025815-2 (lib. bdg.)
ISBN 0-06-440312-2 (pbk.)

First Harper Trophy edition, 1990.

To my husband, Jim,
always my favorite kid next door—
and to Foster and Ruby Smith,
who did such a lovely job of raising him.

While my characters and settings are works of fiction, I would like to express my gratitude to the terrific students and wonderful staff of Park Tudor School, Indianapolis, Indiana.

A special thank-you to those, past and present, who through joy of life, sense of humor, or general eccentricity blessed me on occasion with much needed inspiration:

Jane Holt (who single-handedly kept my children at school on those days they were determined to come home sick!), Jean Magel, Barbara Rominger, Marianne Schafer, Susan Tennant.

Susan Batt, Sam Brandt, John Compton, Kyle Covert, Nisha Garg, Vicki Enlow, Brad Millington, Noelle and Chloe Page, Ben Schafer, Christa Shoot, Andy Singer, Alexis Steinrauf, Scott and Lara Taylor, Mike Tushan, and Cameron Zentz.

And of course, my own resident eccentrics, Bryan and Jaymi.

Acknowledgment

This book was completed with the aid of a Master Fellowship Grant from the Indiana Arts Commission and the National Endowment for the Arts, as well as a Jane Tinkham Broughton Fellowship from the Bread Loaf Writers' Conference.

I am grateful for their support.

Contents

THE
SHOW-AND-TELL
WAR

Starting Up

Adam Joshua didn't mind school, but it always came when he least expected it and usually when he had the most to do.

It was back.

He wasn't ready.

He had planned to do a lot of things this summer, and none of them were finished yet. Some of them weren't even started.

For one thing, he and his best friend, Nelson, had planned to do a bunch of things to the tree house they shared together. Adam Joshua wasn't exactly sure what all of them were, but he knew they would have gotten around to most of them sooner or later.

Also, Adam Joshua thought, he had wanted to work more at teaching his dog, George, tricks. George had a long way to go before he knew most of the things a dog was supposed to know.

Adam Joshua stopped thinking and looked around his room for George. His closet door was open, and George was in there, buried in the piles on the floor, chewing on toys and having a terrific time.

Adam Joshua crawled in the closet too, and started unburying George. There was a crayon on one of the piles, and Adam Joshua scooted the rest of the pile over so he'd have room to sit on the closet floor and make a list on the closet wall.

"TREE HOUSE," he wrote. "GEORGE."

Adam Joshua thought. He wrote "AMANDA JANE" on the list, because his baby sister needed to learn about as much as George, and it was up to him to teach her.

"WRITE A BOOK," he added. He had never told anybody he wanted to write a book, but he did. He always thought he'd use one summer to do it, but he hadn't yet.

"THINGS TO DO NEXT SUMMER," he wrote at the top of his list so he wouldn't forget which list it was. Then he took three comic books off the top of George, took a Space Spy from his mouth, dragged him out of the closet, and slammed the closet door.

Adam Joshua went up to the tree house to see if Nelson was there. He thought if he told Nelson the way he was feeling about school, maybe he'd feel better about it.

Nelson started talking the minute Adam Joshua showed up.

"It's not that I mind school, Adam Joshua," Nelson said. "I even like school. But I had a lot of things I thought I'd do this summer, and there's only a week of summer left and I haven't done most of them yet."

Adam Joshua started to say something about his list.

"And," Nelson went right on, "I've really been worrying about starting school. There are a lot of things to worry about."

Adam Joshua hadn't gotten around to worrying yet.

"For instance," said Nelson, "I'm scared to death that Zed Davis will be in my class again. Last year he kept taking my milk money and pouring glue in my desk, and once at recess he sat on top of me until the bell rang."

All of a sudden, Adam Joshua felt awful. He'd forgotten that he had to worry about a boy named Elliot Banks being in his room again this year.

"And," said Nelson, "I'm terrible at math, especially anything that has a six in it. It seems to me," he said, shaking his head, "that they use more sixes every year.

"Then," said Nelson, "I know we're not going to get to be together, because we never get to be together, and I'm worried about the kind of teacher I'm going to get."

Nelson stopped to take a breath, and Adam Joshua started to say something.

"But most of all," said Nelson, "I'm really going to miss my fish."

Adam Joshua hated Nelson's fish, but he could understand that Nelson might miss them.

Because he was going to miss George.

"I feel a lot better now," Nelson said, watching Adam Joshua climb down the tree-house ladder. "Was there anything special you wanted to talk about?" he asked.

"Not a thing," Adam Joshua said, going back into his house so he could put a few more lists on his closet wall.

George slept on Adam Joshua's stomach each night, and each night Adam Joshua told George the things that he worried about most.

Once in a while George listened, but usually he fell asleep.

In the nights before school started, George slept through Adam Joshua's worrying about a lot of things. Adam Joshua worried about his *L*s the way Nelson worried about sixes. Every time Adam Joshua wrote an *L*, it seemed to turn around the other way, which didn't bother him at all but seemed to bother teachers quite a bit.

"I'm going to get another teacher like that," Adam Joshua told George. "Someone who's going to worry about *L*s all the time." Last year he'd had two teachers. The first was Mrs. Thomas.

"And she was great," Adam Joshua told George, "but then she moved, and Mrs. Lucas came." George slept with his ears flopped down low over his eyes. Adam Joshua lifted one of them up to make sure George heard this part.

"Mrs. Lucas was awful," he said. Mrs. Lucas looked mad all the time, mostly at him. Mrs.

POW

Lucas yelled all the time, mostly at him. Mrs. Lucas thought Elliot Banks couldn't do anything wrong and that Adam Joshua couldn't do anything right. Adam Joshua didn't think he could take another year with somebody like Mrs. Lucas.

"Or Elliot Banks, either," Adam Joshua said, lifting George's ear again.

Elliot Banks was the kind of kid teachers loved and kids hated. Elliot Banks had plenty of money and all kinds of toys, and he was smart in every subject and used the sort of manners adults thought were great.

"A lot they know," Adam Joshua told George.

The worst thing about Elliot Banks was that he hated Adam Joshua, so all last year Adam Joshua had had to put up with being hated.

Between Mrs. Lucas and Elliot Banks, Adam Joshua had spent a lot of time down the hall in the bathroom, sitting on the floor and talking to a spider who lived up in a corner of the ceiling.

"I don't know what I would have done without her," Adam Joshua told George. "Her name was Alice, and she was nearly as good at listening as you are."

George started snoring.

Above Adam Joshua's bed was a poster of his favorite hero, Superman. Adam Joshua planned to be as much like Superman as he could when he grew up. He thought they were pretty much alike already.

They both had muscles, and they both were brave, and one of them could handle anything that came along.

Superman had an archenemy named Lex Luthor.

Adam Joshua had an archenemy named Elliot Banks.

Adam Joshua didn't think Superman had really ever needed to go to school a day in his life.

"He only went to keep everybody else happy," Adam Joshua told George. He fell asleep thinking that he was only going to school to keep everybody happy too.

After breakfast, the first morning of school, Adam Joshua packed his backpack.

He put in pencils and scissors and a ruler. He packed paper and a folder to hold his papers. He put in three of his favorite *Superman* comics and several of his Space Spies and a banana. He stuffed his Superman cape down on top of everything else so he could get to it in a hurry in case it was needed, and he pushed everything down with his foot until he could get the zipper closed.

Adam Joshua went to say good-bye to Amanda Jane. She was sitting in her high chair, banging a cup with one hand and a spoon with the other. In between the banging she was eating pieces of banana and apple, and throwing pieces of cereal down to George, who was waiting for them beneath her high chair.

"I'm leaving now," Adam Joshua told her. "I don't want you to cry."

Amanda Jane reached out and banged him on the head with her spoon.

"I'm going to be in school all day," Adam Joshua told her, "but I don't want you to worry."

Amanda Jane leaned over the edge of her high chair and threw two pieces of cereal down to George. Adam Joshua bent to talk with George and tried to find a clean place to sit.

"I know it's going to be awful without me here," Adam Joshua said. George pushed his nose against Adam Joshua's knee to get at a piece of cereal.

"But I want you to be brave about it," said Adam Joshua.

George growled and bit at Adam Joshua's pant leg, trying to get the cereal.

Amanda Jane leaned over from her high chair and dropped a piece of banana in Adam Joshua's ear.

Adam Joshua hugged his mother and hugged Amanda Jane and kissed George.

He stood with Nelson to look at the tree house for a minute, and then they turned their backs on it to begin the walk to school.

A teacher they knew named Mrs. Worth was standing at the front door of the school with a welcome tag on her shirt and a clipboard in her hand.

"Well, Adam Joshua and Nelson," she said. "Hello, and welcome back! You're exactly two of the people I need to see.

"Adam Joshua," she said, running her finger down the list of names on her clipboard. "You're to be in Room Six. And Nelson, let's see," she said. She looked for Nelson's name.

Adam Joshua stood close to Nelson, and they both held their breath.

"This is terrible," Mrs. Worth said, looking serious. "An awful thing!"

"What?" Nelson whispered, looking scared.

"You're in the same class," Mrs. Worth said, laughing. "Somebody's going to have to put up with you both all year long!

"You'd better hurry," Mrs. Worth said, keeping out of the way while Adam Joshua and Nelson jumped around and hollered and pounded each other on the back, "and see if you can get seats together before the crowd arrives."

Room 6 was nearly empty when they got there.

"This is great, Adam Joshua," said Nelson, picking a desk in the middle of the room.

"Well, it is great, Nelson," said Adam Joshua, picking a desk beside him.

"I wish it wasn't room number six, though," Nelson said. "I'm a little worried about that."

Other kids started coming in the door.

"That's Jonesy," Nelson said, waving at a tall, thin boy, who waved back.

"He's funny," Nelson said, "you'll like him a lot."

"That's Daniel," Adam Joshua said, pointing to a boy who walked in the door holding a book over his head. A girl walked in behind him, trying to bonk him, but hitting the book instead.

"And that's Eleanor Peters," said Adam

Joshua. "She hits all the time, but usually she just hits Daniel."

"There's Gabby," Nelson said, standing up to wave. "Her name is really another name," Nelson said, sitting down again, "but everyone calls her Gabby because she talks all the time. In fact," said Nelson, shaking his head about it, "you're not going to believe how much she talks."

"Alex," said Adam Joshua, waving.

"Sidney," said Nelson, waving.

"Mary Ann," said Adam Joshua, waving.

"There's Angie," Nelson said, waving. "She loves hamsters, and she raises them, but last year her hamsters kept dying."

"Nelson," Angie called, "Wilbur Four died, but now I've got a new hamster! I've named him Wilbur Five!"

"I've always been very happy," Nelson whispered, "that she doesn't raise fish."

Zed Davis didn't show up.

"But Adam Joshua," whispered Nelson, pointing at the door.

Standing in the door smirking around was Elliot Banks. When he saw Adam Joshua, his smirk got even smirkier.

Adam Joshua sighed and scooted down and put his chin on the desk.

A girl Adam Joshua didn't know came by with a green marker.

"Hello," she said, "I'm Martha. I do tattoos for a quarter."

Adam Joshua had never had a tattoo before.

"It's a nice way to start the year," said Martha. "And I can do a tattoo of a pet or a hobby or anything you'd like."

Adam Joshua's mother had given him a quarter to buy a drink at lunch. He could either have milk or a tattoo of George.

"Hold very still," Martha said as she drew on Adam Joshua's arm. "This takes a lot of thought."

The drawing looked a little like a dog, but not a thing like George.

"What do you think, Adam Joshua?" Nel-

CAT

son asked, holding up his arm after Martha had gone, taking both their quarters. "Does that look like a fish to you?"

Adam Joshua thought it looked more like a loaf of bread than a fish, but he didn't want to hurt Nelson's feelings.

"Well," said Nelson, turning his arm to look at it from another direction, "I'm not that crazy about milk for lunch anyway."

A tall, pretty woman walked into the room and smiled.

Everyone quieted down and kept their eyes on her. The woman walked to the blackboard and started writing.

Everyone kept on keeping their eyes on her. Adam Joshua thought her mouth looked like the type that laughed more than it yelled, but he wasn't sure you could be sure about things like that.

"Good morning," the woman said. "I'm your new teacher, and this is my name."

Adam Joshua looked at the board. It was the longest name he had ever seen in his life.

"It's probably the longest name you've ever seen in your life," the teacher said, laughing.

Everybody nodded.

"So I want you to call me Ms. D.," the teacher said. "Think you can handle that?"

Adam Joshua sighed with everyone else and nodded. He thought he could handle that fine.

"Okay," said Ms. D., "get out paper and pencils and let's get busy." Adam Joshua stuck his hand in his backpack so he could get his paper and pencil and get busy. He came out with a handful of squished banana.

"We'll start with some math review," said Ms. D.

Adam Joshua carried his backpack down the hall to the bathroom and dumped everything out. He washed off his pencils and washed off his Space Spies and tried to wash off his comic books. He threw away the banana peel and his paper. When he washed off his cape, the tattoo of George got wet, and George ran off his arm and down the drain.

He stuffed everything into his backpack still wet so that he could hurry, but on his way out the door he looked up into the corner and stopped dead in his tracks. There was a spider up there watching him. It was a different bathroom than last year, so he didn't think it could be the same spider, but it seemed to him it looked just the same.

"Alice?" he said, after a minute.

Alice didn't say anything, but he thought she looked happy to see him.

"I'll talk to you later," Adam Joshua whispered, hurrying back to his room.

"It's all sixes," Nelson whispered, leaning across to lend Adam Joshua paper. "Sixes, sixes, sixes," he moaned.

They had a math review and a spelling review and a review of everything else Ms. D. could think up.

"For this day only," Ms. D. told them, "you may change your seats. If you have a neighbor with habits you don't admire, come talk to me about it," she said, "and we'll try to find a place where you'll feel more comfortable."

Adam Joshua had been noticing a lot of things about Nelson. Nelson hummed sea songs when he wrote, and puckered his lips to make little smacking noises like a fish when he was thinking. Adam Joshua had never been that quiet beside Nelson before and he had never noticed those habits, but now that he had, they were driving him crazy.

Hanah went up to Ms. D. and whispered in her ear. Ms. D. nodded and wrote something on a piece of paper.

When Hanah sat down, Eleanor, beside her, glared.

"By the Beautiful Sea," Nelson hummed.

During study time, another girl and a boy named Philip went up to talk to Ms. D.

Nelson puckered his lips and made fish noises.

"I'll be right back, Adam Joshua," Nelson whispered. He hummed his way to the bookshelves at the side of the room.

Adam Joshua couldn't take Nelson anymore.

While Nelson was busy at the bookshelves, Adam Joshua went up to talk to Ms. D.

"Nelson has bad habits," he whispered, "and I want to move, but he's my friend and I don't want to hurt his feelings."

"That's fine, Adam Joshua," said Ms. D., making a note about it. "We can manage that."

"Fishes, and wishes," Nelson was humming when he got back.

After reading, Ms. D. got out her list.

"Okay, everybody," she said. "We're going to do some scooting around.

"I'd like Philip and Mary Ann to change places, please," she said, "and Angie and Daniel, and Martha and Robert.

"Let's see," Ms. D. said, checking her list, and looking around the room. "Adam Joshua," she said, "I know you're happy where you are, but would you please change seats with Hanah?"

"Oh, Adam Joshua," Nelson whispered, "that's awful. You have to move."

"It's terrible, Nelson," Adam Joshua whispered, packing.

Everybody changed seats.

Adam Joshua put all of his things into his new desk, and leaned back and smiled at Eleanor across the aisle.

She scowled back.

"Some work now," Ms. D. said.

Whenever Adam Joshua looked up at Eleanor, she was scowling or glaring. Then he noticed she was copying from his paper too.

Adam Joshua moved his paper to the far side of his desk. A hand reached across the aisle and pulled it back. Eleanor growled. Adam Joshua went up to see Ms. D.

"I need to move again," Adam Joshua told Ms. D. "Now. In a hurry."

"Yes," Ms. D. said, sighing. "There does

TATTOS
BY
MARTHA
25¢

seem to be a problem developing back there.

"There's a seat beside Elliot," Ms. D. said. "Why don't you take that?"

Adam Joshua looked back at Elliot. Elliot smiled.

"No, thank you," Adam Joshua said politely. "Somewhere else."

"Well, hello," Gabby said when Adam Joshua took the seat beside her. "This is going to be fun!"

Adam Joshua put his name on a new worksheet.

"Adam Joshua," Gabby whispered, "did I ever tell you about the time my cat, Calamity, ran away and I had to spend the day looking for her?"

Adam Joshua started on the first question.

"Well," said Gabby, "first I looked on Glover Street, and I went to every single door and knocked to ask if they'd seen Calamity. She's very easy to see," Gabby said, "because she . . ."

Adam Joshua reread the first question, because he couldn't concentrate long enough to understand it.

". . . white with black spots, although there's a little brown on her tail," said Gabby. "She's a calico, and only girl cats are calicos," Gabby went on. "I looked that up once to see why, but . . ."

Adam Joshua looked at his answer to the first question and erased it again.

". . . Mrs. Palmer said she'd seen her going north," said Gabby, "but then Mr. Palmer came to the door and said, 'No, it was another cat,' so . . ."

Adam Joshua took a deep breath and covered his ears and put his head down on the desk to think about the first question.

"Of course," said Gabby, "I knew Mr. Palmer didn't like cats, so I thought he probably didn't look at them much and wouldn't know Calamity if he saw her, and . . .

"Adam Joshua," she said, watching him pack up, "don't you even want to know what I ended up naming the kittens?"

Adam Joshua moved beside Sidney.

Ms. D. started to hand out vegetable crossword puzzles.

"Uh-oh," Adam Joshua heard Sidney mutter, "this looks like trouble."

The crossword looked hard. Adam Joshua took a deep breath and started on the first row.

"Yep, I was right," Sidney whispered. "Trouble."

"What's red and grows on a tomato plant?" the crossword asked.

"BEET," Adam Joshua wrote. There were two spaces left, so he added two more *E*s.

"A lot of trouble," muttered Sidney. He started to click his tongue and clack his teeth and shake his head and look worried.

Adam Joshua always thought "onion" had an *o* in it, but he had to use a letter from "beetee," so he wrote in "ONIEN."

Sidney clicked.

Adam Joshua tried to think of something yellow that grew underground.

Sidney clacked.

Adam Joshua tried to think of something green and round that came in a pod.

Sidney moaned and groaned, and clicked and clacked, and shook his head so much, he fell out of his chair.

Adam Joshua decided he hated vegetables.

He took his crossword up to Ms. D.

"I need to move again," he told her.

"Adam Joshua," said Ms. D. "This is getting out of hand, and this is it. You choose. Take your time. Look around the room and decide."

Elliot looked up across the room at him and smirked.

"Glad you're back," whispered Nelson, humming away.

Adam Joshua finished his work and sat there a minute. Most people were still working, and he didn't think anyone would miss him. He got up and went to the bathroom. He closed the door and sat on the floor.

"Hi, again," he said to Alice. "I just thought you'd like to know that so far this year I think things are going to be fine."

He sat there thinking about it a minute, and Alice sat there waiting to listen.

"In fact, I think this year is going to be great. Ms. D. isn't the type to yell," he said, "and so far I've known how to do everything she's wanted me to do."

Alice looked like she might be nodding.

"I had a little trouble deciding where to sit, but I've got that worked out. Elliot's in my class, but he's at the back," he said, sighing. "And I guess you can't have everything."

He was pretty sure Alice shook her head.

"So," he said, standing up, "I don't think there are going to be any big problems this year." He opened the door. "See you," he told Alice.

When he walked into the classroom, Elliot was tipped back in Adam Joshua's chair with his feet up on Adam Joshua's desk. Everyone else was gone.

"Last recess," Elliot said, smiling. "So I told Ms. D. I'd stay here and tell you. But what I really wanted to tell you," Elliot said, still smiling, "is that I've got my eye on you."

Elliot poked his finger into Adam Joshua's stomach.

"So don't pull anything," he said, poking with each word. "And don't get in my way."

Adam Joshua hadn't been planning to get anywhere near Elliot.

"That's all," said Elliot, banging the chair to the floor and going out the door to recess.

Some of Adam Joshua's papers were back from Ms. D. Elliot's footprints were all over them.

"Great!" Ms. D. had written across the top paper in red. "Except for your *L*s. Please see me about some practice sheets."

Adam Joshua dug his wet, wrinkled Superman cape out of his backpack, tied it on, and wore it down the hall.

"There may be a few problems," he told Alice.

The Sick Day

Right in the middle of reading one morning, Adam Joshua started to think about George.

George, he thought, was probably missing him very much right now.

George, he thought, was probably hiding, so that Amanda Jane wouldn't try to eat him, and hiding so Adam Joshua's mother wouldn't make him go outside to play, and feeling like nobody in the world loved him at all.

"I know that dog," thought Adam Joshua, and he drew a picture of George in the corner of his reading paper with his paws up over his nose and his ears down over his eyes and dog tears running down his chin.

In the middle of writing, Adam Joshua decided that maybe he wasn't being fair about Amanda Jane. If she was trying to eat George, it was probably because she was feeling lonely too.

Adam Joshua had only been in school a few weeks. Amanda Jane was used to having him around. She wouldn't know what to do without him.

Adam Joshua drew a picture of Amanda Jane in the corner of his writing paper. She was looking out from behind the bars of her crib, sad and blue.

By science time, Adam Joshua was wondering what went on at home all day when he wasn't there to see it. He was pretty sure Amanda Jane and George were sitting around missing him, but he was beginning to wonder if they might be having a lot of fun without him there instead.

George, in fact, might be having so much fun with Amanda Jane that he would decide to become her dog.

On his science worksheet he drew a picture of Amanda Jane and George walking off together, leaving Adam Joshua standing alone.

It took up half the page.

"Adam Joshua," said Ms. D., handing back papers after recess, "your pictures are very nice, but they don't belong on your worksheets." She looked him over closely. "Aren't you feeling well?"

Adam Joshua had been thinking that he wasn't feeling well at all.

"I think I'm sick," he told Ms. D. "I think I'd better go home now."

Ms. D. put her hand on Adam Joshua's head and felt it.

"No temperature," she said. She had him stick out his tongue. "Not green."

Adam Joshua looked her straight in both eyes.

"Green has nothing to do with it," he said.

Adam Joshua went home right after lunch. His mother put her hand on his head and had him stick out his tongue, and sighed at him the same way Ms. D. had.

"Okay, Adam Joshua," she said. "Into bed with you and we'll see what develops."

Adam Joshua wasn't exactly sure what she had in mind, but he thought he'd better work on it.

"If you'd like," he told his mother, "you can send George in here. Amanda Jane too," he said. "I wouldn't mind at all."

"Adam Joshua," his mother said, tucking him in tight, "absolutely not. You're home from

school sick, and you're in bed sick, and babies and dogs shouldn't be around sick people."

Adam Joshua meant to say something to that, but his mother left the room and closed the door on him before he had the chance.

He lay in the bedroom by himself and worked on getting sicker. He tried coughing, and he tried sneezing, and he held his stomach for a while to see if it wanted to hurt. Superman kept watching him from his poster on the wall, but Adam Joshua pretended not to notice.

He could hear giggling coming up the stairs from the living room. He crawled out of bed and crept down the stairs to see what was going on.

He couldn't believe it.

Amanda Jane was sitting in the middle of the floor with George's ears in her mouth, and George was just lying there smiling and letting her eat him. Every so often, George would lick Amanda Jane's stomach where her shirt rode up. And every time he did that, Amanda Jane would burst out laughing.

"Hey!" yelled Adam Joshua, scaring them both. "You can't do that," he shouted, taking George's ears out of Amanda Jane's mouth and wiping her stomach off and pulling her shirt down tight.

"Even if I'm at school, this is my dog," Adam Joshua hollered, picking up George. "Even if I'm sick, it's my dog!" he yelled.

"Adam Joshua," his mother said, from behind him. "Give that dog back to that baby and get yourself back to bed."

"George is my dog," Adam Joshua told his mother, "and she's not allowed to have him."

"Nonsense," his mother told him. "George is the family's dog, and Amanda Jane can play with him as much as she'd like."

"But . . . " Adam Joshua howled, holding tight to George.

"No buts," said his mother, and before he knew it, Adam Joshua was back in bed with the door closed, without George, and he could hear giggling coming up the stairs again.

Adam Joshua crawled out of bed and went to the door of his room. He inched it open and whistled.

No George.

He kept his feet in his room, but he moved his head and stomach out to lie on the floor in the hall.

"Here, George," he whispered.

George didn't come.

Adam Joshua inched farther out into the hall, but he kept his toes in his bedroom to play fair.

"George!" he whispered louder. He heard Amanda Jane laughing. "George!" Adam Joshua yelled.

Adam Joshua's mother picked him up by the neck of his pajamas with one hand and by the seat of his pajamas with the other.

"Scoot," she said, standing there while he

scooted and waiting until he closed the door behind him.

"And you're to stay there," he heard his mother say, on the other side of the door.

———

Adam Joshua stayed there. He inched the door open, and he sat and listened to Amanda Jane giggling and to Amanda Jane chuckling and to Amanda Jane laughing out loud.

And then it got quiet. Too quiet.

Suddenly the door of the room pushed open, and Amanda Jane crawled across his floor as fast as she could and got one of his Space Spies.

Adam Joshua couldn't believe his eyes. He'd always worried that Amanda Jane came into his room while he was away at school and got into his things. He'd always told his mother to be sure to keep his door closed and not let her into his room. He'd always told Amanda Jane to keep out, and he'd always told George to keep an eye on her to make sure she did.

Now Adam Joshua saw that George was

keeping an eye on Amanda Jane just like he'd told him. George trotted into the room right behind her and picked up a Space Spy in his mouth too.

Amanda Jane and George turned around and saw Adam Joshua. George dropped the figure out of his mouth and lay down on the floor and whined. Amanda Jane took one look at Adam Joshua and clamped her teeth down harder on the Space Spy and tried to crawl out the door faster than she came in. Adam Joshua took a flying leap out of bed and tackled her. Amanda Jane hit her chin on the floor, and Adam Joshua hit his head on the door, and George crawled under the bed, and Adam Joshua found himself staring into his mother's knees.

"Feeling better?" his mother asked. She picked up Amanda Jane and checked her chin and stopped her crying. Then she glared down at Adam Joshua.

"They're not supposed to come in my room by themselves," Adam Joshua yelled, crawling

back into bed fast before his mother got around to picking him up by the seat of his pajamas again.

"Never!" he shouted as she left carrying Amanda Jane.

"Ever!" he hollered as George crawled out from under his bed and went sliding through the door without once looking back.

Adam Joshua wiped the Space Spies off on his pajama top and moved all of them to the top of his dresser. He put the stuffed rabbit that had been sitting there down where the Space Spies had been. He thought about it a minute and put it in the closet instead. He didn't think Amanda Jane could crawl with a stuffed rabbit in her mouth, but you never could be sure about Amanda Jane.

He got back in bed and lay down. He was feeling sicker by the minute.

"Adam Joshua," said his mother, coming through the door, "Nelson came by to see you."

Adam Joshua sat up and straightened out his covers to get ready for Nelson.

"I sent him home," his mother said, "because you might be contagious."

Adam Joshua lay down again.

"Nelson brought your books," said his mother, laying a pile of books down on the bed, "and all the schoolwork they did after you left today. Ms. D. sent all the assignments for tomorrow, too, in case you're still sick.

"I thought that was very nice of Nelson," said Adam Joshua's mother, handing him a pencil. "Now you can catch up, and that will make you feel better. Don't worry," she said, "I'll keep George out so you won't be bothered." And she went out the door, closing it behind her.

Adam Joshua looked out the window and saw Nelson's window shade go down and Nelson's hand go up in front of it to start writing.

Adam Joshua got out his binoculars.

ADAM JOSHUA.
ARE YOU OK?
I'M WORRIED ABOUT
YOU

"ADAM JOSHUA," the hand wrote, "ARE YOU OKAY? I'M WORRIED ABOUT YOU."

Adam Joshua got his markers and pulled down his shade and crawled up under it. He drew a picture of himself with his tongue hanging out. He colored his face green and his feet yellow, and he drew red spots and blue dots all over his body.

"GETTING WORSE," he wrote.

"MS. D. MADE GABBY SIT ALONE IN THE CORNER SO SHE COULD GET HER WORK DONE." Nelson drew a picture of Gabby quiet in a corner.

Adam Joshua was sorry to have missed that.

"ANGIE'S NEW HAMSTER DIED," Nelson wrote.

Adam Joshua wasn't surprised.

He waited while Nelson wiped his shade clean.

"ELLIOT BANKS GOT IN TROUBLE TODAY," wrote Nelson. "MS. D. EVEN YELLED AT HIM."

Adam Joshua couldn't believe he had missed Elliot Banks's getting in trouble with Ms. D., and hearing Ms. D. yell at him.

"AND," finished Nelson, "WE HAD A BIRTHDAY PARTY."

Adam Joshua hadn't known there was going to be a birthday party.

He had to wait to find out whose birthday it was while Nelson wiped his shade again.

"HANAH'S," wrote Nelson. "WE HAD CHOCOLATE CUPCAKES."

Adam Joshua loved chocolate. He went back over to look through his books, because he thought if Nelson brought those, he might have brought a cupcake, too. He couldn't find one.

He crawled up under his shade and looked out. Nelson was gone, but a new note said:

"YOUR MOTHER SAID YOU WERE TOO SICK FOR CHOCOLATE. SHE SAID I COULD EAT IT," Nelson had written. "SO I AM."

"Adam Joshua," his mother called the next morning, "it's time to get up and get ready for school."

Adam Joshua had already decided that he wasn't going anywhere.

"Adam Joshua," his mother said, stopping by his room, "you seem fine. I really think you need to go back today."

Adam Joshua coughed. He'd decided on the cough, and he'd been practicing. It sounded awful.

"Young man," his mother said, sighing and feeling his forehead with her hand, "this is it. By noon it's either school or the doctor. You can't plan to stay home forever."

That's just what Adam Joshua *had* been planning. He thought he was maybe going to have to stay home from school forever. There was no telling when he could trust Amanda Jane and George so that he could leave again. He hoped he wouldn't have to be sick and keep coughing and stay in bed forever too, but he supposed if he had to, he would.

He watched out his window Nelson getting dressed and getting ready for school. Nelson came over and pulled down his shade and started writing.

"I'D BE SICK WITH YOU, BUT I'D MISS THE FIELD

TRIP. IF YOU'RE SICK TOMORROW, I'LL STAY HOME THEN." The hand under the shade waved goodbye.

Adam Joshua had forgotten all about the field trip. The whole class was going to the planetarium to look at stars.

Adam Joshua loved stars.

He sighed. Altogether, it seemed to him that it was going to be a long day.

He played a game by himself and he sang a song to himself and he told himself a joke. He'd already heard it.

He read a book, and finally he got bored enough to start on his schoolwork.

All the schoolwork was the same kind of schoolwork he usually worked on all day in school. But at school everyone else was working on it at the same time, and Ms. D. was always around to help. Now Adam Joshua was going to have to do it all by himself, and he wasn't sure his mother knew about any of this stuff in case he got stuck.

He started on his math.

He was on his second row of problems, when he started thinking about everybody at school doing math. He wondered if Nelson was having trouble and needed him there and if he was getting worried about sixes.

He drew a picture in the corner of his math paper of Nelson looking scared with sixes all around him.

Adam Joshua could hear things happening downstairs.

He went into the hall and listened. They were already playing together. He could hear George licking and Amanda Jane laughing.

Adam Joshua slipped down the stairs and pounced on George and pulled his ears down over his eyes and dognapped him before George or Amanda Jane could say anything about it. He took George upstairs and put him in the corner with his blanket, Fred.

"I've got to work," he told George, "so you'll have to play by yourself. But you'll feel better," he said, "knowing I'm here."

Adam Joshua worked on his last row of math. George went along the edge of the bed, trying to find a place to climb up. Adam Joshua kept his leg and foot moving to keep George down.

"Go play in your corner," Adam Joshua said, "and when I'm through working, I'll come play with you."

George didn't listen. He backed up and took a giant leap and flew over Adam Joshua's leg and landed in the middle of the paper.

"George!" howled Adam Joshua.

He took George and put him in the corner, and he took a desk chair and put it on one side of George. He dragged the rocking chair out of Amanda Jane's room to put on the other side of George. Then he stuffed clothes and toys under the chairs and on top of the chairs and all around the chairs to make a high fence so that George couldn't get out.

"Now you'll be fine and feel safer," he said. "You just play, and call if you need me." Adam Joshua went back to work.

He was about through copying his math paper over when George started whining. He wasn't much further along when George started howling.

"Okay, okay," Adam Joshua sighed, picking up all his work and moving it off the bed and over onto the floor beside the chairs. He lay on his stomach and worked his feet through the clothes and toys until they were inside where George was. George settled down to biting and licking Adam Joshua's toes, and Adam Joshua settled back to work.

"Just so you're happy," he muttered to George.

George pounced on Adam Joshua's toes and growled at them and bit on them until he fell asleep. Things in the room got quiet.

Adam Joshua started his science. They were studying planets and stars. Adam Joshua was one of the best people in the class when it came to knowing about stars. Ms. D. called on him to answer questions about stars all the time.

He couldn't believe she'd take everybody to the planetarium to look at stars without him.

He drew stars around the edges of his paper, and he drew the school bus with Ms. D. and everybody in it. Everybody looked terrible because Adam Joshua wasn't along to tell them about things, and Ms. D. looked like she was going to cry.

Just then, Adam Joshua heard Amanda Jane crying.

He ignored her for a while, but it began to sound like she was sobbing. Adam Joshua couldn't figure out where his mother was, because she ought to be doing something to help. He had never heard Amanda Jane cry like that before.

He pulled his feet carefully out from underneath George and went downstairs. Amanda Jane was lying in the middle of her toys, howling as though her heart would break.

Adam Joshua lay down beside her and patted her back. Amanda Jane didn't care. She kept right on howling.

"Adam Joshua," his mother said, kneeling beside them, "where on earth is George?" She picked up Amanda Jane and bounced her to see if that would help. "Amanda Jane and George play together at this time of the day. She loves him and she's used to him and she needs him. She's lonely," said his mother.

Adam Joshua felt terrible. He hadn't known Amanda Jane felt like that about George.

"Adam Joshua," his mother said, sitting down in a rocking chair to rock Amanda Jane, "George is full of love. He can love Amanda Jane during the day and you at night, and still have lots of love and energy left over. He can be a dog that belongs to both of you," she said, "and it will never matter one bit."

Adam Joshua wasn't sure about that, but it didn't seem to him that he had any choice.

Amanda Jane was still howling when Adam Joshua carried her upstairs to her crib.

She kept right on howling until Adam Joshua brought George and put him in the crib with her.

Then Amanda Jane cheered up right away. She put her head on George's side and his ear in her mouth, and fell asleep making chuckling little baby noises.

Adam Joshua watched them for a minute. It made him feel terrible, but not as bad as he thought it might.

The bus was leaving for the planetarium right after lunch. Adam Joshua hurried back to his room and dug under the bed for the clothes he'd worn two days before.

He didn't have all his work done for today, but he thought Ms. D. would be so happy to see him she wouldn't mind.

He took two of his oldest Space Spies off the top of his dresser, and he dug for some rope in a drawer. He went into the hall and closed the door of his room. He tied one end of the rope around his doorknob and the other end around the leg of a table that stood in the hall.

"NO TRESPASSING," he wrote on a sign, and he put it on the floor so it would be low enough

NO TRESPASS-
ING

for Amanda Jane and George to read.

Then he put his Space Spies by the sign so that when Amanda Jane and George woke up and found he'd gone back to school, they wouldn't miss him too much.

The Library Caper

One of the things Adam Joshua liked best about school was the library.

One of his favorite days was library day.

"This is it," Ms. D. told everybody. "The library's open, and Mrs. Jackson's waiting for us."

Mrs. Jackson waved at everyone as they came in, and sat at her desk ready to check books out.

Nelson headed straight for the fish books. Philip headed straight for the books on space. Gabby headed straight for Mrs. Jackson to talk for a bit. And everybody else headed straight for the books they liked most.

Adam Joshua looked at mysteries and he looked at books about dinosaurs and he looked at the books about famous people.

"Hurry up, Adam Joshua," Ms. D. said. "Everybody's almost ready."

Adam Joshua looked at books about things in the past and books about things in the future, and he found a book on how to build a rocket.

"Adam Joshua," Ms. D. said, "everyone else is through."

Adam Joshua started across the room to check the rocket book out, but on his way there something caught his eye. It was a fat red book stuck down behind a lot of other books, and he wasn't sure because he couldn't see much of it—but what he could see looked like a picture of Superman's foot.

"Adam Joshua," Ms. D. said, behind him.

"You go on ahead," said Adam Joshua, pulling books off the shelf to get to the book behind. "I'll be there in a minute."

Adam Joshua worked until he could see Superman's legs, and he took books out until he uncovered the whole book with a picture of Superman flying fast across it.

"Why, Adam Joshua," Mrs. Jackson said, "we've been looking for that book a long time. Everybody loves that book," she said, "but one day it disappeared."

Everybody crowded around, and Adam Joshua held up the book for them to see.

"I don't suppose," said Mrs. Jackson, "that you'd mind being the first to check that out?"

As far as Adam Joshua was concerned, he didn't mind at all.

Adam Joshua read the book about Superman during writing, and he read during science time, and he read during math until Ms. D. came and took the book away.

"I know just how you feel," she whispered, "but you can get your book back after school and take it home to read."

"Adam Joshua," said Nelson, as they walked home after school. "You can't even see where you're going." He pulled at Adam Joshua's sleeve to keep him from walking into a tree. "Superman's just not worth it."

"He's worth it," Adam Joshua said, looking up from his book long enough to show Nelson. "Here he's fighting and here he's flying and here," he said, "he's making things safe for everyone."

Nelson looked at the book with Adam Joshua and they both walked into a fire hydrant.

At home, Adam Joshua closed his bedroom door to keep people and babies and dogs out, and he curled up on his bed to read.

"Pow!" he whispered, reading about Superman.

It was the best book he'd ever had. It told all about Superman being born and about

Superman coming to earth and about all the things he had done here since he came.

"Come play," Nelson yelled from the tree house outside Adam Joshua's window.

"I can't," Adam Joshua yelled back. "I'm reading now."

"Superman wouldn't want you to be like this," Nelson shouted.

Adam Joshua pulled the window shade down and curled up again on his bed. "Double pow!" he whispered.

Adam Joshua took the book about Superman back to school and let Ms. D. keep it until recess.

"Look," he said then, showing everybody everything.

"Pow!" everybody said, looking at the way Superman did things and then running around trying to do them too.

"It's a bird, it's a plane!" Alex yelled, swinging the swing high and jumping out and landing flat on the ground.

"Able to leap tall buildings in a single bound!" Jonesy yelled, jumping over Alex.

"Adam Joshua," said Angie, "I just love that book."

Everybody but Nelson nodded. Everybody but Nelson loved it too.

"Library day," said Ms. D. "Time to check books in and check books out."

Adam Joshua didn't even stop at the book-shelves. He walked straight to Mrs. Jackson's check-out desk and handed her *Superman.*

"Again," he said, getting out his pencil to sign the card.

"Adam Joshua," Mrs. Jackson said, laughing, "we've got a problem. You must have been showing that book around a lot and getting everyone excited about it. Just look at this waiting list."

Adam Joshua looked at the waiting list for *Superman.*

Philip's name was on the list, and so were Daniel's and Eleanor's. Martha was waiting for *Superman,* and so were Alex and Jonesy. Nelson's name was there along with everyone else's.

"That's not fair!" yelled Adam Joshua. "Nelson doesn't even like Superman," he hollered. "He shouldn't get the book!"

"Adam Joshua," said Mrs. Jackson, "it's fair. Maybe Nelson wants to learn more about Superman to see if he likes him. That's what books are for."

"But this is my book," said Adam Joshua. "I love it."

"It's Hanah's turn, Adam Joshua," Mrs. Jackson told him. "Hanah is sick today, but her brother's going to stop by after school and take it to her. If you'd like, you can put your name on the waiting list too."

Adam Joshua didn't like it at all, but it was what he had to do.

"ADAM JOSHUA," he wrote at the bottom of the list.

"In a couple of months it will be yours again," Mrs. Jackson told him, taking *Superman* away and laying it on the corner of her desk.

"Adam Joshua," she called after him, "don't you want to check out another book at all?"

Adam Joshua went down the hall to the bathroom, and he shut the door and sat on the floor.

It was quiet and lonely, and Alice was up in her corner waiting to listen.

"You wouldn't believe it," Adam Joshua told Alice.

He could hear people going past in the hall, talking about their books.

Adam Joshua and Alice sat, staring eye to eye.

Adam Joshua didn't blink. The spider didn't blink.

"Adam Joshua," Ms. D. called.

Adam Joshua let Alice win and went back to the room. He glared at Nelson.

"Adam Joshua," said Nelson, looking up from the book he was reading, "what did I do?"

Adam Joshua sat in his chair and looked

around. Almost everybody was reading. Angie was reading a book called *Healthy Hamsters and How to Have Them*, and Jonesy was reading a book called *The World's Worst Jokes.* Gabby was gabbing away. Nelson was reading about whales.

"Excuse me," Adam Joshua said to Ms. D., who was reading her book too. "But I have to go back to the library. I forgot something."

"Mmm," Ms. D. said, turning a page. "But hurry."

Adam Joshua hurried. He went to the door of the library and looked inside. Mrs. Jackson was nowhere in sight. Adam Joshua could see the *Superman* book still lying on the desk across the room.

"Very slow," he whispered, "very quiet." He tiptoed up to the first row of bookshelves and crouched low and stuck his head around it fast. No Mrs. Jackson. Adam Joshua crouched low and stuck his head around the second row of shelves, and then around the third.

Mrs. Jackson was down at the end of the

SPACE
Read

row putting books back in their places.

Adam Joshua waited until her head was turned, then scurried past the book aisle and zoomed up and grabbed *Superman* off the desk. Mrs. Jackson was still looking the other way when Adam Joshua tiptoed back by.

"*Superman* again?" Nelson asked, glancing up as Adam Joshua slipped the book out from under his shirt. "I'm waiting for that book too," said Nelson, holding his own book up higher so he could get a better look at a picture of a big blue whale.

Adam Joshua stuck *Superman* deep into his book bag and didn't take it out again the whole time he was at school. When he got home, he put it far under his mattress the very first thing.

"Don't worry about it," he told George, when they lay in bed that night looking at *Superman* under the covers with a flashlight.

"They'll never even miss it," he said.

They were just starting reading the next

morning when Mrs. Jackson stopped by.

"I'm sorry to disturb you," she told Ms. D., "but I have an announcement to make. It's very important."

"Well, if it's important," Ms. D. said, smiling, "then go right ahead."

"A terrible thing has happened," Mrs. Jackson said, looking around the room to see if everybody was listening.

Everybody was.

"I think we've had a thief in the library," Mrs. Jackson said, and everybody gasped. Adam Joshua started sliding down in his chair.

"The *Superman* book has been stolen," Mrs. Jackson said. Adam Joshua kept on sliding.

"After Adam Joshua turned the book in," Mrs. Jackson said, "I put it on the corner of my desk. And not long after that," she said, "someone took it off."

Adam Joshua's chin was resting on his desk, and he couldn't get any farther down.

"If any of you know anything about this," Mrs. Jackson said, "please come see me. This is a terrible thing."

People were looking at Adam Joshua. They were looking suspicious.

"This is awful!" he shouted, standing up. "How could somebody do a thing like that?" He waved his arms and looked his worst. "That book is important. We really needed it!"

"Poor Adam Joshua," he heard someone whisper. "It was his favorite."

"Oh, no!" he heard Nelson whisper.

"Excuse me," Adam Joshua said, going out the door and down the hall to sit on the bathroom floor.

Adam Joshua ran all the way home after school.

"Cookies," his mother called. Adam Joshua hurried on by. Amanda Jane threw a ball at him to play, and George galloped up to lick his shoes, but Adam Joshua didn't even see them.

He locked the door of his bedroom and pulled the book out from under the mattress

AMANDA
JANE
SUPERMAN

and sat staring at it for a long time. When he looked up, Nelson was watching him from his bedroom window.

Nelson's shade went down. A hand with a marker went up under the shade and started writing.

"ADAM JOSHUA," the hand wrote, "WHY DIDN'T YOU WAIT TO WALK WITH ME AFTER SCHOOL? ADAM JOSHUA," it wrote, "I WANT TO TALK TO YOU."

Adam Joshua got up and pulled his shade down tight.

He pulled the covers down on his bed and crawled under them and held *Superman.* A while after that, he crawled down to the foot of the bed and lay under the covers alone in the dark.

He couldn't figure out what to do. Crying wasn't going to help, but he did that while he was thinking. He should give *Superman* back, he knew that. But if he gave *Superman* back he knew he'd never get to get it as much as he needed it. He thought if he explained that to someone, then maybe everyone would understand, but he couldn't think of anyone he could even tell.

He gave up thinking and just cried.

He couldn't give *Superman* back.

He needed it.

Superman was all anybody talked about at recess the next day.

It was a thief from outside, everybody said. Nobody at school could have done a thing like that.

"And he might be back anytime," said Sidney. He was trying to carry everything from his desk around with him at recess so the thief couldn't get at it.

"Adam Joshua," said Martha, "you must feel really awful. You really loved that book."

Adam Joshua looked at the ground and nodded.

"I loved that book too," said Mary Ann. "And I was fourth on the list."

"I was third," said Nate, "so I'm really mad."

"I wouldn't get it till seventh," said Gabby, "but I could hardly wait, and I would have loved it, and now I'll never get it at all."

"People," said Ms. D. after recess, "the *Superman* book is still missing. It's important," she said, "for anyone who knows anything about it to tell what they know."

Everybody shook their heads to show that they didn't know a thing.

Adam Joshua and Nelson didn't even look at each other.

"It's a very old book," Ms. D. said, "and we can't replace it. There are no copies left of it to buy," she said.

Everybody shook their heads to show how bad that was.

Adam Joshua and Nelson kept right on not looking at each other.

"We need everyone's help," said Ms. D.

"I know who the thief is," Elliot said, raising his hand. "And I intend to catch him for you any day."

Adam Joshua felt the back of his neck go cold.

"That's fine, Elliot," Ms. D. said, "but I imagine whoever took the book will solve the problem himself. I don't think you need to try catching anybody."

"We'll see," Elliot said, with a low chuckle that Adam Joshua felt along his neck from clear across the room.

That afternoon Elliot followed Adam Joshua home from school. He went along the edge of the sidewalk, hiding behind trees, thinking Adam Joshua wouldn't see him.

Adam Joshua saw him. Farther down the sidewalk he saw Nelson, too, walking slowly along behind, watching them both.

At home, Adam Joshua pulled out *Superman* and crawled under his covers down to the foot of his bed. He couldn't give it back. But any day now Elliot was going to catch him or Mrs. Jackson was going to come along and throw him in jail.

If he could buy it somewhere, he thought, he would, but he couldn't because Ms. D. said there weren't anymore around.

He had every book about Superman they'd ever had at the bookstore, but he'd never been able to get a book like this before.

So he wouldn't give it back, he thought.

"Don't worry about it," he told *Superman.*

Even when they came to take him to jail, he was going to hide the book and take it to jail right along with him.

He lay there for a while and thought about going to jail.

He thought Amanda Jane and George could come and see him on visiting day, but he wasn't sure it was a good idea for a sister that age to see her brother in jail, and he knew it would make George sad. He knew Nelson would come visit him, which was nice of Nelson, but he didn't think they could stay best friends. It would be hard to play games or build things that way, he thought, wiping his eyes and nose on the sheets.

He thought about his mother and father having to come see him in jail, and that thought made him start crying so hard he fell out the end of the bed.

"Do something," Adam Joshua told *Superman* as he lay on the floor in a tumble of sheets and blankets and book.

Superman didn't come, but it didn't matter. Lying there, after a long time of crying, Adam Joshua thought of what he could do himself.

"HAVE YOU SEEN THIS BOOK?" a poster in Mrs. Jackson's library asked the next day. There was a drawing of the book on it, and drawings of a sad Mrs. Jackson and mad kids standing around.

During the day Nate and Jonesy and Angie drew on the poster to make the kids look worse.

During the day Adam Joshua watched until the library was empty, and he ran up to the poster and stuck a note on it fast.

"WIJJ BE COMING SOON," said the note. "DON'T WORRY ABOUT A THING."

That afternoon Adam Joshua hurried home.

Elliot hurried after him.

Nelson hurried behind them both.

"I'm sorry, but you have to leave," he told George, giving him a kiss on the chin, and shoving him out the bedroom door.

Adam Joshua got out stacks of paper and all his markers and all the crayons he could find that George hadn't been chewing on.

He could see out his window Elliot standing down on the sidewalk watching his house, but Elliot couldn't see in, so Adam Joshua left the shade up.

Adam Joshua lay on his stomach on the floor and started to copy the book. He wanted a cover just like the cover on the book, so he used cardboard and wrote "SUPERMAN" across the top and drew a picture of Superman flying. Superman looked lopsided and lumpy, and it took forever to color him in.

"One page finished," he finally said, standing up to stretch. He looked out the window and looked right at Elliot looking in. Elliot was

MARKERS
CRAYONS
GLUE
HAB
CHIPS

in the tree house taking jumps in the air, trying to see what Adam Joshua was doing on the floor. Nelson was sneaking up on Elliot, and the last thing Adam Joshua saw before pulling the shade down was Nelson tackling him.

The next morning everyone was gathered around the poster in the library.

"The note must be from the thief," Angie said, "but what does it mean?"

Everybody shook their heads. Nobody knew what it meant.

"That thief," Hanah said, looking the note over closely, "makes his *L*s just like Adam Joshua."

People crowded in to see. Mrs. Jackson looked at Ms. D., and Ms. D. looked at Adam Joshua along with everybody else.

"Lots of people," Nelson said, in a hurry, "make their *L*s like that. Why, that's something," he nearly shouted, "that I've seen all the time."

Martha carried a poster up and hung it on

the wall beside Mrs. Jackson's.

Adam Joshua thought it was supposed to be a picture of Superman. It looked more like a flying tomato with a nose.

"I did this for free," said Martha, giving her poster a pat. "With something like this, everybody's got to do their part."

Adam Joshua had worked on copying *Superman* the night before until he got put to bed. After he'd gotten put to bed he waited until everyone else had gone there too, and then he'd gotten up to keep working.

There were 157 pages to copy. He'd only made it to page 11 before he'd fallen asleep on the floor. He'd been so tired, he barely made it up in time to leave for school before Nelson.

He started yawning during reading, and he yawned during writing, and he yawned through lunch.

After lunch, Adam Joshua slipped back to the empty library. A new note was on Mrs.

Jackson's poster.

"PLEASE HURRY," said the note. "PEOPLE ARE WAITING!"

"I AM HURRYING," Adam Joshua wrote. "IT JUST TAKES A LITTLE TIME."

"Don't worry. It's not Adam Joshua," Hanah told everyone later. "The thief has learned to change his *L*s around, so it can't be him at all."

Adam Joshua fell asleep during math. It wasn't until Nelson started growling about sixes that he woke up.

"Adam Joshua," Ms. D. said, at recess, "I'm worried about you. You're looking very tired."

"Adam Joshua," yelled Angie, after she'd thrown a ball that hit him on the head, "if you're going to play this game, you have to pay attention!"

"Adam Joshua," said Nelson, following him around the playground. "I want to talk to you!"

Adam Joshua was the first back into the room. The papers and books and Space Spies from his backpack were scattered all over his desk. He'd packed his Superman cape neatly that morning and now it was thrown on the floor.

"THE BOOK'S NOT HERE, BUT I KNOW YOU TOOK IT!" a note lying on top of his backpack said.

"What happened to your stuff, Adam Joshua?" Nelson asked, coming in from recess with everybody else.

"Nothing," Adam Joshua muttered. He shoved the note to the bottom of his backpack, and he pushed everything else in on top of it. His cape was crumpled and one comic was ripped and his Superman pencil was missing.

Adam Joshua looked on top of his desk for the pencil and then in his desk, and then he started walking around his desk to see if his pencil had fallen to the floor.

"Do you have a problem there, Adam Joshua?" Ms. D. asked.

Elliot was sitting at the back of the class writing with Adam Joshua's pencil. He looked up at Adam Joshua and smiled.

"No problem," Adam Joshua told Ms. D., picking his cape up off the floor and folding it to pack away too.

On his way home, Adam Joshua saw Elliot, but he didn't see Nelson.

He was pretty sure he was going to lose Nelson as a friend. He thought maybe he should start worrying about that, but he was already so worried about *Superman*, he didn't think he could worry about Nelson, too.

He knew as soon as he had time to worry about Nelson, he was going to feel terrible.

But when Adam Joshua opened the door of his bedroom, Nelson was sitting there holding the *Superman* book in one hand and the copies Adam Joshua had been making in the other.

Adam Joshua didn't say anything.

"Your mother said I could come on up," Nelson said, "so I did."

Adam Joshua didn't say anything.

"These are terrible Supermans," said Nelson. "They're awfully lumpy. I draw much better," said Nelson, "and I've got better markers. I'll go get them," he said. "Then I'll be back to help."

Adam Joshua watched Nelson walk out the door. He put his backpack down, and stood looking at the 146 pages of copying left to do.

"Thank goodness," he said.

Each day after school, Adam Joshua and Nelson went up to Adam Joshua's room to copy *Superman.*

Each day, George got kissed on the chin and shoved out the door.

"Adam Joshua," said Nelson, rubbing his hand and rubbing his eyes. "We're not even half done. We're not even a third done," he said, "and I don't think I can draw anymore. I'm not sure this is a good idea."

"Nelson," said Adam Joshua, "it's the only idea I've got. If we copy the book," he said, "then I can take the book back and keep it

too. Nelson," he said, "if I take the book back, I won't have to go to jail."

"They don't put kids in jail," Nelson said. He watched while Adam Joshua got up to peek out under the window shade and check on Elliot. "I don't know what they do, but they don't put them in jail."

Adam Joshua hadn't realized that.

"They might do something worse," Nelson said, starting to color in Superman's feet.

Adam Joshua hurried back from the window and started copying.

Each night after bedtime Adam Joshua would sneak out of bed to copy *Superman*.

Some nights Nelson was able to sneak over to help. Other nights Nelson sat at home in his room by his window so that Adam Joshua wouldn't feel alone.

They both yawned through reading and yawned through writing and fell asleep during math.

"Boys," Ms. D. said, "what on earth is making you so tired?"

"Boys," Angie said, after she'd hit them both on the head with the ball, "will you please pay attention!"

"We could always hire Martha," Nelson said, stacking copied pages in a pile and counting the pages left to copy. "If you wouldn't mind Superman looking like a flying tomato with a nose," he yawned.

"Finished," Adam Joshua whispered to himself late one night as he finished the last page.

"FINISHED," he wrote on the back of his shade, and he held the flashlight under the shade so that Nelson could see.

When Nelson didn't answer back, Adam Joshua flashed his light at Nelson's window.

Nelson was sitting there keeping Adam Joshua company, sound asleep with his head against the glass.

Adam Joshua wiped his and Nelson's fingerprints off the book and packed it deep at the bottom of his backpack.

He crawled in his closet and found his "THINGS TO DO NEXT SUMMER" list. "WRITE A BOOK" was on the list. Adam Joshua crossed it out.

"NEVER AGAIN," he wrote beside it.

George was sound asleep, waiting outside Adam Joshua's door. Adam Joshua picked him up and put him in bed. He crawled in beside him.

George crawled up on Adam Joshua's stomach without lifting an ear or opening an eye.

"Never again," Adam Joshua muttered at George, without opening an eye either.

"I'll keep Elliot busy at recess," Nelson said on their way to school. "I'll ask him about the things he owns. He loves to talk about his things."

While everyone was out at recess and Elliot was telling Nelson all about his things, Adam Joshua slipped up to Mrs. Jackson's desk and left *Superman* on the corner.

"THANK YOU VERY MUCH," said Adam Joshua's note. "SORRY TO HAVE BEEN SO LONG."

" 'Bye," Adam Joshua said, standing there for a minute looking at *Superman.* Then he turned his back on it and walked away.

"It's over," he told Alice, going in to sit on the bathroom floor. "I'll probably feel terrific about it later," he said.

Alice looked like she probably agreed.

"In fact, I probably feel the best I've ever felt," said Adam Joshua.

Alice probably nodded.

"It's not the same, though," he told her. "My book looks a lot the same, but it still isn't the *Superman* book. There'll never be another book like that," Adam Joshua said.

He didn't even try to stop the tears dripping down his cheeks.

Halloween

As far as Adam Joshua was concerned, Halloween made everyone a little batty.

His father went around the house wearing a wobbly fake nose and his mother went around cackling a witch's cackle and Nelson hung out his window each night to howl at the moon.

Adam Joshua spent a lot of time dressed like Dracula, but it wasn't easy. His fangs hurt and his cape kept getting caught on bushes and people kept biting him back.

At school, everybody kept trying to scare everybody else.

"The next person who jumps out and tries to bite my neck is going to get it," Angie said.

Adam Joshua put his fangs back in his pocket.

"And I'm really getting sick of knock-knock bat jokes," said Ralph.

Ms. D. hung cobwebby stuff on the door so they had to walk through it to get to their classroom each day. She went around humming songs about goblins, and she kept them busy decorating.

They cut out pumpkins from orange paper and witches from black paper. They hung them above their desks.

"Enchanting," Ms. D. said, looking around the room.

"If you don't mind my saying so," Martha said, going by and tipping her head back to look at Adam Joshua's things, "your pumpkin is lopsided."

"And your witch is lumpy too," Nelson said from across the aisle.

Sidney opened his desk top and screamed at a black fake spider someone had put there.

"Halloween really makes me nervous," he said.

Adam Joshua's class went on a field trip to get pumpkins.

"This is great!" Gabby said, taking a seat beside Adam Joshua as everyone piled on the bus. "I can tell you about all my Halloweens!"

"Are there snakes in pumpkin fields?" Sidney asked, looking worried.

"Who said there were snakes?" Angie said, tucking her feet up underneath her on the bus seat.

"SAM'S PUMPKIN PATCH," a sign said when they got to the pumpkin field. A farmer named Sam was there to meet them.

"Glad you're here," said Sam, helping people down from the bus. "Just take your pick."

"Choose from the small pumpkins," Ms. D. said, showing them where the smaller pumpkins were. "Otherwise, we won't have room."

Eleanor bopped Daniel and two other people on the head getting to the pumpkin patch, and she stepped on two pumpkins and broke them on her way.

"Easy," said Sam, leaning on the gate. "The pumpkins aren't going anywhere. Just take your time to choose the one you like best."

Adam Joshua took his time. He liked his pumpkins best with a lot of character. He walked past round, fat pumpkins, and he walked past tall, thin pumpkins, and finally in a corner of the pumpkin patch he found a lopsided pumpkin that looked like it could be somebody nice.

"Adam Joshua, are you sure you want this pumpkin?" Ms. D. asked, holding it up to look it over closely. Everybody else crowded around to look it over closely too. Everybody laughed.

"I'm sure," said Adam Joshua, taking it back again, and patting it on its lopsided side.

"Good e-ven-ing," a creaky voice said behind them.

When they all turned around, Dracula was there.

"Good e-ven-ing, yourself," Ms. D. laughed. "I'm surprised to see you out and about at this hour."

Dracula threw back his head and howled, and everyone who had been laughing about the pumpkin got quiet in a hurry.

"Special times for special people," said Dracula, smiling at them so his long white teeth glistened in the sun. He took Adam Joshua's pumpkin and held it up.

"This pumpkin," said Dracula, testing his teeth on it, "has a lot of character. This pumpkin," he creaked, "is just the one I'd choose."

Everybody nodded.

Adam Joshua got out his fangs.

"I'll be right there," he told Ms. D. while

SAM'S PUMPKIN PATC

everyone headed for the bus.

"Thank you ver-ry much," moaned Adam Joshua.

"You're ver-ry welcome," moaned Dracula.

"Have a nice Hal-lo-ween," Adam Joshua creaked.

"Same to you," Dracula creaked back.

Adam Joshua said good-bye to Dracula with the secret vampire handshake.

"See you later, Sam," he said, scurrying to catch up with the rest of the class.

Back at school, everybody lined their pumpkins up on newspapers and got out their paints and got out their brushes and got ready.

"Okay," said Ms. D., "draw a face on the pumpkin first. Then you won't be as apt to make a mistake."

"And if anybody needs any help with their pumpkin, please see me," said Martha.

Philip drew a long, mean-looking face on his long, mean-looking pumpkin, and Mary Ann drew one with high eyes and tall teeth and a wicked, fat nose. Hanah had a plump, round pumpkin so she drew a plump, round face and she put in dimples.

Adam Joshua could only get one eye drawn on his pumpkin, and if he put in a nose there was only room for two tiny teeth.

"It looks awful," Adam Joshua said, showing Ms. D.

"Well, Adam Joshua," said Ms. D., "I've loved a lot of one-eyed pumpkins in my life. It doesn't look so bad."

Ms. D. helped Adam Joshua squeeze an extra eye in next to the first one, and she helped him draw the nose smaller and the teeth bigger.

"This pumpkin is a masterpiece," said Nelson, patting his pumpkin on the head as Adam Joshua went back by. "This pumpkin is a work of art."

"Okay, everyone start painting," said Ms. D.

"I hate art stuff," said Sidney.

Adam Joshua painted one perfect eye.

"I did it!" he yelled.

He started painting the second eye, but first the paint dripped down to the nose, and then it made a river into the second eye. By the time Adam Joshua was through fixing it, the eyes ran together to make one big eye, and the nose had gone off to one side and had run down to where the mouth should have been.

Adam Joshua turned his pumpkin around to the back, and painted the mouth there.

"That's a very unusual pumpkin, Adam Joshua," said Hanah, finishing up a dimple.

"Adam Joshua," said Nelson, "that pumpkin's ridiculous."

"We're going to have a Halloween party," said Ms. D. "And we're going to have a lot of fun.

"For your costumes, come as something scary," Ms. D. told them. "In fact, I want you to choose a costume of something that scares you the most."

Adam Joshua drew pictures on the edge of

his math paper of the things that scared him the most. He drew the real Dracula with blood dripping off his teeth. He drew a werewolf howling at the moon. He drew skeletons tap-dancing on their graves.

"Nice pictures," the note from Ms. D. said when he got his math paper back, "but they don't belong on your worksheets. See me."

Adam Joshua waited till recess and went up to see Ms. D.

"Adam Joshua," she said, "your ideas about the things that scare you are good, but they're ordinary. Try to think of the things that might not bother anyone else, but still get to you. The private frights," she said, laughing and giving him a hug.

"It's too bad I can't dress like a six," Nelson said at recess. "It would help Ms. D. understand about that."

Ms. D. handed around art supplies, and they cut out bats from black paper and ghosts from white paper and hung them up.

"Bewitching," Ms. D. said, looking around the room.

"Lopsided," said Martha on her way by.

"Lumpy," said Nelson.

"If anyone needs any help with their costumes," Martha wrote on the blackboard before leaving, "please see me."

Before bed, Adam Joshua cut bats from black paper and a snowman from white paper.

"I like snowmen," he told George. He cut ghosts from green paper because he'd used up all the white.

He hung everything up.

"Bewitching," he told George.

He lay on his bed and tried to think about what scared him so that he could figure out what to be for Halloween.

"Got any ideas yet?" he asked George.

The longer he lay there thinking, the more things he thought up. He hadn't known there were so many.

He tried to decide what scared him most.

He wasn't crazy about elevators, poison ivy, big horses, big dogs, or little bugs. He hated brussels sprouts, long underwear, and washing his hair.

He was scared of rats, bats, the worst kinds of snakes, kryptonite, and going to the dentist.

He was scared of ever stealing anything ever again.

He thought about dressing like Elliot Banks. But then Elliot Banks would know just how scared Adam Joshua was of him, and that would be really scary.

There used to be a monster who lived in his third dresser drawer. Adam Joshua had been scared to pieces of *that.*

He was pretty sure the monster was gone, and he was pretty sure he wouldn't be afraid of it anymore even if it wasn't gone. But after he had been lying there awhile thinking about it, he slid George off his stomach, got out his baseball bat, and creaked open his third dresser drawer to make sure.

NELSON
HIS FISH

On his way back to bed, he saw Nelson at his window. His face had red stripes and black stripes, and his hair was sticking out in points all over his head.

Adam Joshua didn't have the faintest idea what Nelson was trying to be, but whatever it was, he was doing a very good job of it.

Nelson raised his window and leaned out.

Adam Joshua opened his own window and listened to Nelson howling. Adam Joshua howled back.

Nelson's mother showed up in Nelson's room at the same time Adam Joshua's mother showed up in his. Adam Joshua let out a final howl as his mother tucked him tightly in bed, and he could hear Nelson doing the same.

He decided on the monster. He was a bit worried that people might think he was acting like a little kid, afraid of a monster. Still, if it had been their monster, they would have been shaking in their boots.

By the time his costume was together, Adam

Joshua scared himself every time he looked in the mirror.

He looked exactly like the monster from his third dresser drawer, and he wasn't exactly sure he was happy about it.

His mother had made him a brown fur suit, and the suit had floppy, wicked ears. He wore claws on his fingers and claws on his toes and his Dracula teeth. He tied on a carrot for a nose.

Every time George saw Adam Joshua, George started howling. And every time George howled, Adam Joshua tried to kiss him and the carrot got in the way.

When Adam Joshua opened the door to let Nelson in, George left the room altogether.

"I'm a shark, Adam Joshua," said Nelson, taking the vampire teeth out of his mouth. He had on blue pants and a blue shirt, cardboard flippers on his arms, and a big cardboard shark fin on his back. He wore his swim flippers on his feet and his swimming mask over his eyes.

"I know sharks are fish, Adam Joshua," said

Nelson, "and normally I love fish. But I'm scared to death of sharks."

Nelson's flippers kept falling off as he walked, and Adam Joshua kept losing his claws along the way.

"Did you know sharks eat most of the other fish, Adam Joshua?" Nelson asked, walking back to get a flipper and picking up two claws for Adam Joshua. "They don't even care what the other fish think about that.

"I can't believe it," Nelson said, when they walked into their classroom and looked around. Adam Joshua shook his head along with Nelson. He couldn't believe it either.

Daniel was dressed in blue pants like Eleanor Peters always wore and a striped shirt like Eleanor Peters always wore, and he had on a wig with hair a lot like hers, and he wore glasses like hers without lenses.

"ELEANOR PETERS," a sign around his neck said.

"Hey!" yelled Eleanor Peters. "That's not the least bit funny!"

ELEANOR
PETERS

She bopped Daniel on the head.

"It doesn't hurt so much this way," he told Adam Joshua. "You'd be surprised how much the wig helps."

Nate was dressed up in yellow and black, with two cardboard wings on his arms and two pipe cleaners stuck to a headband on his head.

"I'm a bee," said Nate, flapping his arms and buzzing and nodding his head so that the pipe cleaners bounced.

"I'm terrified of bees," he said. "Once a bee started to eat my sandwich at the same time I was, and it stung me on the tongue. A thing like that," he said, shivering, "can make you scared for a long time."

"There are a lot of things people don't know about sharks," Nelson was telling everybody. "People would be scared to death if they knew."

Philip was dressed in brown and was trying to slither around on the floor like a snake.

"If real snakes have this much trouble," he said, after Adam Joshua had tripped over him and Nelson had walked on him and Eleanor Peters had stomped on him, "then I'm going to switch from being scared of them to feeling sorry for them."

Sidney looked ridiculous. Adam Joshua thought Sidney looked like he'd put on a little of everything he could find in the house.

"It looks a little confused," Sidney said, "but I worry about a lot of things, and I started to worry I'd leave some of them out."

"I'm surprised," Nelson said as they took their seats, "that there aren't more people dressed up like sharks."

"Who's first?" Ms. D. asked.

Everybody suddenly looked shy. Nobody wanted to go first.

"Those of you who want to," said Ms. D., "can come up and tell us about your fear. But some of you may not think it's especially necessary. You can just tell us you're a secret fear. That's all we need to know."

Eleanor Peters stomped up with three cook-

ing pots clattering from her belt and two eggbeaters dangling from a string around her neck.

"I'm a secret fear," she said, bopping Nate on his pipe cleaners on her way by, "and nobody'd better say a thing about it."

Angie had on a bald head and a big nose, and plastic claws on her fingers, and she was wearing a lot of green.

"I'm a space alien," Angie told everyone. "I've seen a lot of those shows about space aliens coming, and they scare me to death. Does anybody think that's funny?" she asked.

Everybody looked at everybody. Everybody shook their heads. Nobody thought that was funny at all.

"Well, that helps," said Angie, going back to her chair. "It's nice to know that other people worry about those things too."

Jonesy had on a sheet he had dyed gray. The sheet had clumps of gray-colored tissue glued on it and black round spots stuck on.

"Oatmeal," said Jonesy, turning around so

they could see all sides. "With raisins," he said.

"Jonesy," sighed Ms. D., "you did a good job of looking like oatmeal. But Jonesy, you were supposed to come like something you're afraid of."

"I'm really scared of oatmeal," said Jonesy, peering out from under his sheet. "Every time my mother makes me eat it, it scares me to pieces. Does anyone think that's funny?" he asked.

Everybody looked at everybody. Everybody burst out laughing.

"That's what I thought," said Jonesy, laughing too, and walking back to his chair with pieces of raisins falling on the ground behind him.

Hanah was dressed like a spider. "It's more that I hate spiders than that I'm scared of them," she said. "I smack every spider I see. I've been trying to get that one on the ceiling of the girls' bathroom for ages," she said, "but I always miss."

Adam Joshua got up right away to go check on Alice.

"Hi," he said, peeking in the bathroom door. "Don't be scared, it's me." Alice didn't say anything, but Adam Joshua didn't think she looked like she'd been in the girls' bathroom nearly getting smacked.

"Have a happy Halloween," he said.

When he got back to the room, Elliot was going to the front, just dressed like himself.

"I don't have any fears," he said. "I sure don't have any baby fears about things with carrot noses." He smirked at Adam Joshua.

Ms. D. frowned at Elliot. "Adam Joshua," she said, "would you like to come up now and tell us about you?"

Adam Joshua thought about it in a hurry. He didn't think it was especially necessary.

"I'm a secret fear," he said, turning around in front of the class so they could see him anyway. "That's all you need to know."

Ms. D. stood up and turned around for

everybody. She was dressed all in black, with wispy black material on her arms and head, and a black cape down her back.

"I've not told many people," she said, "but I thought you would like to know. All my life—" Ms. D. turned around again so that the cape and material floated around her—"I've been scared of the dark. Even now," she laughed, "I sleep with the light on."

"Ms. D.," Eleanor Peters said, standing up, banging and clanging her pans and beaters, "that's ridiculous. Grown-ups aren't afraid of the dark, and I don't think teachers are allowed to be."

"Eleanor Peters," said Ms. D., "please sit down. Just because you're an adult doesn't mean you get over what scares you. You outgrow some of your fears, and some you keep. The ones you keep," she said, starting to hand out napkins for the doughnuts and cider, "you just get along with as best you can."

That night Adam Joshua and Nelson went

trick-or-treating. The moon was fat and yellow. Plump little clouds scurried across the sky and crunchy leaves scurried across the street, and Adam Joshua and Nelson scurried along the sidewalk, looking over their shoulders.

"Adam Joshua," Nelson sighed, "every year you're afraid of things hiding in bushes, and every year it takes us a long time to get our candy because you take so much time going the long way around all of them."

"But things do hide in bushes, Nelson," Adam Joshua said. "Lots of things. Ghosts. Werewolves. Dracula."

"Adam Joshua," said Nelson, "some of the houses we never even get to. We miss out on a lot of candy because of your dumb bushes."

Adam Joshua scooted out to the edge of the sidewalk because there was a big bush up ahead.

"Good grief!" Nelson said, walking close to it and shaking the branches to show he wasn't afraid.

A spider, a snake, and a space alien jumped out and pounced on Nelson.

"Your chocolate or your life!" the alien shouted.

"You can't win," Nelson sighed.

"Adam Joshua," Angie said as they picked Nelson up and brushed him off, "we stopped to trick-or-treat at your house, and your mother came to the door dressed like a witch. She cackled a lot."

Adam Joshua could believe it.

"Then your dad came out on the porch with a funny nose on," Philip said, "and he danced a wild and crazy dance."

Adam Joshua was sorry to hear that.

"Don't worry," Hanah shouted as they hurried on their way. "We gave your dad some of our candy so he'd stop."

Nelson went the wide way around bushes the rest of the night.

"It doesn't seem fair," he said on their way home. "We've been getting ready for Halloween for so long, and it just got here and now it's gone. I wish things like Halloween wouldn't do things like that."

He threw his head back and howled at the moon.

"They could have another Halloween instead of Labor Day," Nelson said, heading for his house. "We never get any candy for Labor Day," he shouted back.

Adam Joshua sat on his porch and looked at the moon for a minute. One of the clouds going by looked just like a witch.

Through the window he could see his father dancing a crazy dance. Amanda Jane was in his arms, and she was wearing the funny nose.

Adam Joshua threw his head back and howled at the moon too.

Then he scurried inside his house in a hurry before something out there in the dark howled back.

The Show-and-Tell War

"Tomorrow," Ms. D. told the class, "we're going to start a new kind of show-and-tell. I want it to be the kind of show-and-tell that helps us know you better. So I'd like you to bring the things that help us do that. Bring in things that say a lot about you."

That night Adam Joshua looked around his

room and tried to think of things that would help people get to know him better. He looked at his soccer ball and his stuffed elephant and his model of a dinosaur. It didn't seem to him that any of those had much to say.

He looked at his Superman cape, but he thought the less he reminded people how he felt about Superman, the better. No one had mentioned the stolen book for a long time, but he wasn't taking any chances.

"So not that," he said, opening his closet door and digging through the clothes that were on the floor of his closet and through the games and toys that were under the clothes and finally through the stuff he never used that was down at the bottom under everything else.

Adam Joshua lifted an old blue shirt and a Frisbee that was only half there because George had eaten the other half. Underneath them his old no-legged, one-armed teddy bear was staring up at him with a one-eyed stare.

"Well, hi," he said, hugging his bear. "You've

been gone a long time."

Once Adam Joshua had slept with his bear every night. Once it had been the best friend he'd ever had.

"George does those things now," Adam Joshua told his bear, "but he can't go to school. So, you'll do just fine." He brushed the bear off and gave it another hug, and put it on the dresser beside his backpack so it could start getting used to the idea.

"Everybody's going to love this show-and-tell," Nelson said the next morning on their way to school. He was carrying a box with his books and posters about fish. He was making Adam Joshua carry a box with maps showing where different fish live and a model showing how the inside of a fish looks.

"They're just going to love it," Nelson said, humming a little "By the Sea" while he walked.

"Show-and-tell," Ms. D. said. "Hands up."

Everybody's hand went up.

"Great!" Ms. D. said, laughing. "Ellen, you can go first."

Ellen marched up to the front of the room carrying a baton and a bag.

"These are some of my trophies," Ellen said, taking trophies from her bag and lining them up at the front of the room for everyone to see. "I won them for twirling my baton."

Adam Joshua had never known anyone who had won trophies. He clapped along with everyone else.

"I can throw my baton high in the air and catch it every time," Ellen said, throwing the baton high and catching it with one hand.

Adam Joshua clapped harder.

Ellen threw the baton higher and it came down on her head.

"Usually," she said.

Nate walked to the front of the class with a bag.

"This is Windberg," he said, pulling out a stuffed dog. It had long, floppy ears and a

long, pointed nose and a green sweater.

"He's my favorite thing," Nate said, stuffing Windberg headfirst into the bag and putting it on the show-and-tell table beside Ellen's trophies.

"And I love him a lot," Nate said on his way back to his desk.

Everybody clapped for Mary Ann and Daniel and Nelson.

"Knew they'd love it," Nelson whispered, humming as he sat down again.

"My mother's going to have a baby," Philip told them all during his turn. Everybody groaned for Philip.

"That's just wonderful, Philip," Ms. D. said, calming everybody down.

"That's too bad, Philip," Adam Joshua heard three people whisper as Philip went back by. He thought he'd better have a talk with Philip himself, sometime soon.

"Gabby," Ms. D. said, "show-and-tell should be your thing. Why don't you come up now?"

Gabby walked up smiling, carrying a box. When she turned and saw everybody waiting, her smile faded.

Gabby didn't say a word.

Everybody waited.

Gabby started to twist one foot, and then she started to twist one braid, and finally she began to chew on the other braid.

"Gabby?" Ms. D. asked.

Gabby looked up at the ceiling, and she looked down at the floor, and then she just stood there looking scared to death.

"Maybe you'd like to sit down again?" Ms. D. asked.

Gabby kept her head down all the way back to her desk.

Adam Joshua kept his bear in his backpack until it was his show-and-tell, and then he took it out of his bag and marched it to the front of the room.

"I've had this bear," he said, holding it up, "for a long time. This bear," said Adam Joshua, turning it around so everybody could see it from every angle, "says a lot about me."

Elliot Banks in the back row whispered something to Mary Ann, beside him. Mary Ann giggled. Elliot Banks whispered something to Philip, on his other side. Philip snickered.

Elliot said something a little louder, so that a lot of people heard and a lot of people started laughing.

"People," said Ms. D., "you are being very rude to Adam Joshua. Elliot, would you mind saying what you have to say out loud?"

Elliot came up the aisle holding a box and stood at the front of the room beside Adam Joshua.

Inside the box was a brand-new set of hero warriors, full of muscles and carrying swords and shields.

"These say a lot about me." Elliot grinned, showing them around. "These say I'd never play with a torn-up baby's bear."

A lot of people giggled. Several others started

to hoot and howl.

Ms. D. frowned them all quiet.

"Adam Joshua's bear," Ms. D. said, "looks like it's been loved a lot. I like that. What I don't like, Elliot," she said, "are your manners. I think they could improve."

"Probably," said Elliot, smiling at everybody and going over to make room for his warriors on the show-and-tell table.

Adam Joshua took his one-eyed bear to his desk and stuck it in his book bag way down at the bottom.

"Well, I think that was a great first show-and-tell," he heard Ms. D. saying as he went out the classroom door into the hall.

"And I'll bet tomorrow will be even better," he heard her say as he walked toward the bathroom to talk to Alice.

That night, Adam Joshua lay in bed in the dark and told George all about it.

"It was awful," he said.

WACKOS

He tried to think what he could take the next day for show-and-tell.

He had been thinking about taking a lot of things, but now nothing seemed right.

"We're supposed to bring something," he told George, "but I don't know what."

Just as Adam Joshua was falling asleep, he thought about the picture his great-aunt Emily had given him.

"Why, that will work fine," he told George, waking him up to tell him. "No one will laugh at that at all."

The next day, Angie went first for show-and-tell.

"I have a new hamster," she said. "His name is Wilbur Seven, and he's fine and fat and healthy. I'm going to bring a picture of him tomorrow to show you."

"I can't believe it," Nelson moaned in a whisper. "Not another one!"

Nate walked to the front of the class with a bag.

"This is Windberg," he said, pulling out a floppy-eared, pointy-nosed dog in a blue sweater. "My favorite thing," he said, stuffing it headfirst into the bag again.

"Didn't we see Windberg yesterday?" Ms. D. asked, looking puzzled.

"I had another at home just like him," Nate said, walking to his desk.

Martha came to the front with two pictures.

"I call this one 'Windberg in a Bag,' " she said, looking at Nate.

"And I call this one 'The Moray Eel,' " she said, looking at Nelson.

"Now, these cost only . . ."

"Martha," said Ms. D., "no selling."

"Right," Martha said, nodding. She took the pictures to the show-and-tell table and took a little sign out of her pocket to put beside them.

"50¢ EACH," it said.

"Adam Joshua, would you lend me your milk money?" Nelson whispered.

Adam Joshua waited until Elliot had taken his turn at show-and-tell before he even raised his hand.

"Brand-new," Elliot said, holding up a spaceship full of action figures. "Very expensive," he said.

Adam Joshua tried not to look too interested, but that was exactly the spaceship he'd asked for at Christmas.

"You've got to be kidding," his mother had said.

"And Santa Claus is going to say you've got to be kidding too," his father had said right after.

Elliot walked over and shoved other things to the side and put his spaceship in the center of the show-and-tell table. Everyone else in the room sighed along with Adam Joshua just looking at it.

"This is my great-aunt Emily," Adam Joshua said, holding up his picture, "when she was a little girl growing up in Kansas. In this picture," he told everybody, "they're building a sod house."

"Why, that's a wonderful picture, Adam Joshua," Ms. D. said. "Take it around so everyone can see it."

Adam Joshua took it around, and everybody but Elliot looked it over closely, and everybody but Elliot asked a lot of questions, and everybody but Elliot said they thought it was wonderful too.

"If you like that sort of thing," Elliot said, yawning.

"Let's put it right here, Adam Joshua," said Ms. D., going over to the show-and-tell table and moving Elliot's spaceship to the side to put the picture of Great-Aunt Emily in the center. "That way we can enjoy it all day, if that's all right with you."

Adam Joshua went back to his desk humming. It was perfectly fine with him.

The next day Adam Joshua took in his favorite truck for show-and-tell. It was a nice

BIRD
BY
MARTHA
BOOKS
ARE
GREAT
V. CHESS

truck. It didn't say a lot about him, but he thought it said enough.

Philip went up after Adam Joshua.

"My mother's going to have a baby," Philip said.

"We know. You told us already," Ms. D. said. "It's really nice."

"You told us twice already," somebody said.

"And all the time during recess," said somebody else.

"I know," said Philip, shaking his head and going back to his chair. "I just can't get used to it," he said, sighing and sitting down.

Nate came up with his bag.

"Windberg," he said, pulling a dog from it. "One of my favorite—"

"Nate," Ms. D. said, interrupting. "Just how many Windbergs do you have?"

"Sixteen," said Nate.

"Right," sighed Ms. D.

"My rock collection," said Sidney. "I don't know what it says about me. It seemed like a person should have a collection, so I picked up a bunch of rocks one day and put them in a box."

"You could read and learn about them," Ms. D. said. "I think rocks can be pretty exciting."

"You can have them then," Sidney said, leaving the box on Ms. D.'s desk.

Gabby came to the front of the room and looked at Ms. D. and shrugged.

Ms. D. shrugged back.

"You might try saying 'Hello,' " Ms. D. said.

Gabby took a deep breath and took the braid out of her mouth.

"Hello," she whispered.

Everybody clapped and cheered.

First Gabby looked surprised, and then she looked happy.

"Good-bye," she said, louder, and when everyone clapped some more, she smiled all the way back to her seat.

Elliot went up last, and he went up carrying a big bag and wearing a big smirk. He looked at Adam Joshua, and his smirk grew smirkier.

"My family," Elliot said, looking at Adam Joshua, "has been in America since the beginning. Why, when the pioneers were just pioneering," he said, "my family had been around for years.

"My family crest," said Elliot, taking a wooden board out of a box that had been in the bag. It had a lot of gold on it and some animals and writing Adam Joshua couldn't understand, and a lot of other stuff he couldn't understand either.

"These charts," said Elliot, pulling a rolled-up paper from his bag and unrolling it, "are charts about my family. They show we're related to the king."

Everybody in the class but Adam Joshua went, "Ohhhh!" Nobody had met anybody related to a king before.

"Those are very interesting, Elliot," said Ms. D. Everybody nodded.

"Why don't you put them in the center of the show-and-tell table."

"I had already planned on it," said Elliot.

Adam Joshua had to stay in from recess to practice *L*s. Nelson had to stay in to practice sixes. "Sixes, sixes, sixes," Nelson muttered. "What are you going to do about Elliot and show-and-tell?" he asked.

"L,L,L,J,L," Adam Joshua wrote. "I can't think of anything to do," he told Nelson.

"Well," said Nelson, "I'm your friend, and if you decide what to do about Elliot and you need me to help you do it, just tell me and I'll do it."

He turned one of his sixes into a fish floating across the page with bubbles coming out of its mouth.

"Thank you," Adam Joshua told Nelson. "If I think of something you can do, then I'll tell you."

He tried to turn one of his *L*s into George, but George simply wasn't built that way.

"My trucks," Elliot said the next morning, unfolding a big display case at the front of the room. "Needless to say," said Elliot, "they cost a fortune, and I've got the newest you can buy right here."

"Thank you, Elliot," said Ms. D. "Why don't you put them on the floor beside the show-and-tell table so they don't take up all the space."

Adam Joshua kept his hand down and sat in his chair thinking.

Jonesy walked up looking serious and took a box from a bag and a picture from the box. "My family tree," Jonesy said, holding up a picture of a tree full of monkeys.

Everyone burst out laughing.

"This one," Jonesy said, pointing at a small monkey, "looks especially like my little brother."

Adam Joshua kept right on keeping his hand down, thinking.

Gabby walked up smiling, with her box.

"Hello," she said right away.

Everybody waited.

"Hello," Gabby said a little louder, looking a little more scared.

Ms. D. started clapping, and everyone clapped along.

Gabby smiled. She opened her box and took out a white and brown seashell.

"I thought maybe you'd like to know about this," she said, "because it's one of my favorite things." She waited.

Everyone clapped.

"Well, then," said Gabby, "one time we went to the beach, and my whole family went except for my cat, Calamity. She had to stay home because . . ."

"Uh-oh," whispered Nelson.

". . . and the sun was shining, and the waves were pretty high. I'd say about as high as . . ." said Gabby.

"I knew it," whispered Nelson.

"Of course, I've always liked sand," said Gabby, "except for the kind that sticks when . . ."

"I just knew it," muttered Nelson, scooting

SMILE
SEE
SEA
SI
SHELLS

down in his chair and putting his head on his desk to take a little nap.

"Adam Joshua?" said Ms. D. "We haven't heard from you."

"I forgot today," Adam Joshua said, leaving his harmonica in his backpack. "I'll try to remember tomorrow," he said.

"That will be fine," said Ms. D.

"What about your harmonica, Adam Joshua?" Nelson whispered. "You played it all the way to school this morning."

"Later, Nelson," Adam Joshua whispered. He could feel Elliot staring a hole in him, but he didn't look in that direction at all.

"It's like this," Adam Joshua told George that night. "Anything I bring," he said, "he's going to bring something just like it that's newer or better or more expensive. So what I need," Adam Joshua told George, "is something that's special, that nobody else could have.

"I'm sorry," he told George, lifting one ear

so he could look in one eye, "but dogs aren't allowed for show-and-tell. Thank you for mentioning it, though," he said.

He could see out his window Nelson's shade going down. A hand wrote on it for a while, and then another hand came back with a flashlight so that Adam Joshua could read it.

"I'LL BRING FISH FACTS FOR YOU TO USE TOMORROW," he read. "YOU CAN CHOOSE BETWEEN DEADLY PIRANHA OR STARFISH."

"If you don't mind," Adam Joshua told Ms. D. the minute he got to school, "I'd like to go last for show-and-tell. I have something special to show," he said, "so I'd like to wait."

"Well, that would be fine, Adam Joshua," said Ms. D.

"Hands up," Ms. D. said at show-and-tell time. "Everybody ready?"

Everybody was ready. Nelson talked about fish, and Philip talked about babies, and Gabby just talked. Jonesy brought in a dead snake to show everybody, but it was so disgusting nobody could look.

"Angie," Ms. D. called, "did you bring your picture of the new Wilbur? We're all anxious to see him."

Angie looked up from her desk and gave her head a sad shake.

"Never mind," she told Ms. D.

Finally only Elliot and Adam Joshua were left.

"I'll wait," said Elliot. "Adam Joshua hasn't had his turn yet. Why doesn't he take his?"

"Adam Joshua and I have already discussed it," said Ms. D. "I'd like you to take your turn now."

Elliot went to the front of the room carrying two bags.

"All of these things," said Elliot, dumping the bags out on the floor, "are mine. All of them are new," he said, glaring at Adam Joshua. "All of them cost a bunch." Elliot looked around the room to make sure most people were pay-ing attention, but most people weren't. Most people looked like they were getting tired of Elliot.

"It's like going to a toy store, Adam Joshua," whispered Nelson. "But even toy stores get boring after a while."

"And I can bring even more tomorrow," Elliot said, glaring at everybody.

"Adam Joshua has a special show-and-tell for us today," said Ms. D., "so everybody sit up and give him your full attention."

Everybody looked at Adam Joshua and sat up to give him their full attention. Elliot was moving things around on the show-and-tell table to make room for his toys. He gave Adam Joshua a look of attention that made his toes curl.

"Adam Joshua," whispered Nelson, "I walked to school with you, but you didn't bring a show-and-tell. You didn't bring a thing that's special."

"That's what you think," said Adam Joshua,

and he stood up and took Nelson's arm and pulled Nelson up to the front of the class with him.

"This," said Adam Joshua, standing Nelson beside him, "is Nelson."

Everybody sat there quiet. Everybody already knew that.

"Adam Joshua," whispered Nelson, looking like he wished he could go sit down again. "What are you doing?"

"Nelson," Adam Joshua continued, "is my very best friend. Having a friend like Nelson," he said, "says a lot about me."

Nelson stood a little straighter and looked a little prouder.

"Nelson and I have known each other for a very long time," said Adam Joshua, "and we built a tree house together, and we fought a war against Nelson's cousin Cynthia together, and we do about everything together anybody could want to do."

"Sometimes we collect old things that have been around," said Nelson. "And sometimes

SHOW
AND
TELL

we build new ones that no one's ever thought up before."

"Quiet, Nelson," said Adam Joshua.

"It doesn't matter what trouble I'm in," said Adam Joshua. "Nelson's always there to help."

Everybody cheered and clapped. Nelson took a bow.

"Adam Joshua," said Ms. D., "that was wonderful."

"That was really something, Adam Joshua," Anita said at recess.

"Once I helped Adam Joshua look for his dog, George, for two hours. And I don't even like George," said Nelson.

"Adam Joshua," said Philip, "that was really great."

"Once I helped Adam Joshua teach George tricks for two days. And I really hate George," said Nelson.

Adam Joshua watched Elliot during recess. Elliot kept running around and grabbing people's arms and talking at them.

"But I don't want to be your friend!" Adam Joshua heard Philip shout.

Ralph came over and stood beside Adam Joshua and shook his head.

"That Elliot," said Ralph, "is going crazy, Adam Joshua. He told me he'd pay me to be his friend. He said I could have one of his trucks and some other stuff. Who'd want a friend like that?" said Ralph.

Adam Joshua watched Elliot pulling at people until he had run out of people to pull at, and then he saw him go in and sit at his desk looking like he was going to cry. Ms. D. was in the room, and Adam Joshua saw her go over and sit beside Elliot. She talked to him for a long time, but Adam Joshua didn't know at all what she had to say.

"I think show-and-tell went very well today, don't you, Adam Joshua?" Nelson said on their walk home.

"Show-and-tell," Ms. D. said the next day. "Hands up."

"Windberg," said Nate.

"And then there was the time I . . ." said Gabby.

"I have a new hamster," said Angie.

"I can't believe it," moaned Nelson.

"Here are pictures of Adam Joshua and me doing things together," Nelson said during his show-and-tell. "Here we're building and here we're swimming and here we are with my fish and George." Nelson looked closely at the picture and then pointed to the fishbowl. "One of my fish is smiling," he said.

Ellen brought Mary Ann to the front of the class.

"Mary Ann is my best friend," said Ellen. "We do interesting things together, like skate and collect and make plans to go to the moon. It's nice to have a friend like that," she said.

Alex brought Philip to the front of the class.

"My best friend," said Alex, pointing to Philip. "He doesn't do much of anything that's interesting," Alex said, "but neither do I, so we're fine together."

Sidney came to the front of the class by himself.

"I don't have a best friend yet," he said. "But I just wanted to say that I like to go to movies, read, and collect rocks. If anybody else here likes to do those things and would like a best friend, I'd be very interested to know it."

Sidney looked around the room and waited for somebody to say something, and when nobody did, he sighed and went back to his seat.

"This is my best enemy," said Daniel, pulling Eleanor to the front of the room. "She hits me all the time and she hurts me all the time and I thought everybody should know." Eleanor looked like she was getting ready to hit Daniel right then, but Ms. D. was watching.

Elliot came last for show-and-tell, carrying a small box. Everybody sat still, waiting to see what was in it.

"It's either something that cost a lot of money," Nelson whispered, "or he finally just brought a box of money."

Elliot took the lid off the box and put it down and stood there looking shy.

"Maybe nobody's interested in this," Elliot said. "But I collect fossils. I've been collecting them for a long time," he said, "and then I read about them and label them."

Everybody was interested. Everybody wanted to see the fossils, so Elliot walked around the room to show them, and everybody had questions to ask and Elliot knew how to answer them all.

"At recess," Sidney said, "I'd like to talk to you about things."

"Come put that right here, Elliot," Ms. D. said, making space in the center of the show-and-tell table. "So everyone can have a chance to really study them later."

Elliot put his fossils in the middle of the show-and-tell table, and when he looked up, he looked at Adam Joshua.

It wasn't very easy to smile at Elliot, but after a minute Adam Joshua did it.

And Adam Joshua knew it couldn't have been very easy for Elliot, but after a minute Elliot took a deep breath and smiled back.